HIDDEN WORLDS

by James Bow

Crabtree Publishing Company

www.crabtreebooks.com

Crabtree Publishing Company
www.crabtreebooks.com

Author: James Bow
Project Coordinator: Kathy Middleton
Editors: Adrianna Morganelli, Tim Cooke
Proofreader: Crystal Sikkens
Designer: Lynne Lennon
Cover Design: Margaret Amy Salter
Picture Researcher: Andrew Webb
Picture Manager: Sophie Mortimer
Art Director: Jeni Child
Editorial Director: Lindsey Lowe
Children's Publisher: Anne O'Daly
**Production Coordinator and
  Prepress Technician:** Margaret Amy Salter
Print Coordinator: Katherine Berti

Photographs
Cover: Thinkstock (middle); Shutterstock (background)
Interior: Corbis: Peter M. Wilson 10; **Getty Images:** Werner Forman 13t; **Mary Evans Picture Library:** 9; **Public Domain:** Nadar 11; **Shutterstock:** 5, 14, 15, 20, 22, 23, 28, Niall Dunne 6, Gert Hochmuth 21, David Hughes 26, Nataliya Hora 17, Alberto Loyo 7, Vadim Petrakov 16, Dmitry Pichugin 29, Anna Subbotina 4; **Thinkstock:** Hemera 24, istockphoto 18, 19, 25; **Topfoto:** 12–13, Fortean 8, 27.

Library and Archives Canada Cataloguing in Publication

Bow, James, 1972-
     Hidden worlds / James Bow.

(Mystery files)
Includes index.
Issued also in electronic formats.
ISBN 978-0-7787-1124-7 (bound).--ISBN 978-0-7787-1128-5 (pbk.)

    1. Civilization, Ancient--Juvenile literature. 2. Antiquities--Juvenile literature. 3. Excavations (Archaeology)--Juvenile literature. I. Title. II. Series: Mystery files (St. Catharines, Ont.)

CC171.B68 2013   j930   C2012-907857-3

Library of Congress Cataloging-in-Publication Data

CIP available at Library of Congress

Crabtree Publishing Company
www.crabtreebooks.com   1-800-387-7650

Published in Canada
Crabtree Publishing
616 Welland Ave.
St. Catharines, ON
L2M 5V6

Published in the United States
Crabtree Publishing
PMB 59051
350 Fifth Avenue, 59th Floor
New York, New York 10118

Published by CRABTREE PUBLISHING COMPANY in 2013
Copyright © 2013 Brown Bear Books Ltd

All rights reserved. No part of this publication may be reproduced, stored in a retrieval system or be transmitted in any form or by any means, electronic, mechanical, photocopying, recording, or otherwise, without the prior written permission written permission of the copyright owner.

Printed in Hong Kong/012013/BK20121102

Contents

Introduction	4
Island of STATUES	6
Hollow EARTH	8
Secret TUNNELS	10
China's Lost PYRAMIDS	12
The Cave TEMPLES	14
Pools of MYSTERY	16
Homes in the CLIFFS	18
Towns of GHOSTS	20
Living UNDERGROUND	22
Life in the CAVES	24
King Arthur's CAMELOT	26
Monasteries of the MOUNTAINS	28
Glossary	30
Find Out More	31
Index	32

Introduction

On September 12, 1940, a French boy named Marcel led some friends into a cave near their village to look for lost treasure. But when the light of their lamps hit a particular wall, they found something greater than any treasure: colorful paintings of deer, horses, and oxen. The boys told their teacher. He called in an expert who found that the paintings were 17,000 years old.

Mystery words...

outcrops: rock formations that stick out of the ground

Hidden Worlds

The story of the Lascaux Caves is an example of rediscovering something hidden. This book will show you other hidden places all around us. There are tunnels that allowed soldiers to sneak past the enemy, and abandoned towns that were once full of people.

Perhaps places became hidden because they were abandoned and forgotten. Perhaps they were deliberately hidden. Or perhaps they were hidden because, even though they were visible, they were almost impossible to reach. Such hidden worlds can give us a better understanding of the visible world around us.

Monasteries in Metéora, Greece, were built high on rocky **outcrops**.

Island of STATUES

Easter Island is one of the most isolated places on Earth. It is 1,290 miles (2,076 km) away from its closest neighbor. But when the Dutch explorer Jacob Roggeveen arrived in 1722, he found a remarkable sight.

Only 3,000 people lived on the island. But gazing over the landscape were hundreds of giant stone heads. The statues were up to 30 feet (9 m) tall and weighed up to 80 tons (73 metric tons). The islanders called these statues *moai*. They used them to worship their **ancestors**. But how could so few people have created them? Well, we now know that only a century before Roggeveen arrived, the island had been home to far more people.

Mystery words...

ancestors: early individuals from whom someone is descended

Mystery File: GREAT BURDEN

Some historians think the *moai* led to the collapse of the Easter Island civilization. Carving the statues took a lot of time. Without being looked after, the land could not support all the people. Eventually many people left the island.

Collapse of an Island

From about 1250 to 1500 A.D., the Easter Islanders carved a total of 887 *moai*. But they were so busy making statues they didn't grow enough food. They cut down all the trees to make rollers to move the statues. Wars broke out among them as they fought over food. The island's population fell sharply as people left. The *moai* were simply left in place, gazing out over their empty lands.

Some moai *were set up in rows on stone platforms.*

Hollow EARTH

These diagrams show a world inside Earth.

Many ancient peoples believed that the center of Earth was hollow. The Greeks believed that the dead dwelled there in huge caverns. In Navajo myth, their ancestors emerged from a cave, fleeing war and flood inside Earth. It took until the 19th century for scientists to prove that the center of Earth is solid.

A ship sinks in a drawing from Journey to the Center of the Earth.

Early scientists suggested that it was hollow under Earth's surface. But in the 19th century, scientists showed that this could not be true. If Earth were hollow, it would have less mass, and **gravity** would be weaker than it is. Today, we know that at Earth's heart is a rocky iron core. Earth's surface is a series of plates that float on layers of **molten** rock.

Mystery File: UNDERGROUND BOOK

In 1864, the French novelist Jules Verne wrote *A Journey to the Center of the Earth*. The novel describes an expedition into an extinct volcano in Iceland. The volcano leads to a world with oceans and storms, but no inhabitants.

The Theory Continues

But scientific proof didn't end the idea that Earth is hollow. Early in the 19th century, John Cleves Symmes argued that there were holes at the poles that led to worlds hidden inside. Even in the 20th century some people still argued that the human race had emerged from inside the Earth, through a large hole at the North Pole.

Mystery words...

molten: melted, used to describe something that is usually solid

Secret TUNNELS

In the 1950s, rebels against French rule in Vietnam began to dig a system of tunnels beneath Saigon, the capital city. They used the tunnels to hide in when they began a military campaign against the French.

By the 1960s, the rebels were known as the Viet Cong. They began fighting U.S. troops based in Vietnam. The tunnel system was 75 miles (121 km) long. It was entered by secret trapdoors. Many of the tunnels were

Reconstruction of a Viet Cong command center

Mystery File:
THE CATACOMBS

Beneath Paris, France, a mile (1.6 km) of tunnels was used in the 19th century to bury the dead. These **catacombs** hold thousands of skulls and other bones. The tunnels were first dug as mines to produce stone to build the city.

The catacombs of Paris were built in old tunnels.

too small for people to stand up in. They connected kitchens, command centers, and **dormitories**. The Viet Cong stayed in the tunnels all day, and came out at night to launch attacks. Conditions were hard. The tunnels were full of ants, scorpions, and venomous centipedes. Virtually all the rebels got sick.

The tunnels gave the Viet Cong an advantage in the Vietnam War. The U.S. Army bombed the area, but failed to destroy the tunnels. Today, the tunnels are a popular tourist attraction.

Mystery words…

catacombs: underground cemeteries located in tunnels

China's Lost PYRAMIDS

China's "lost pyramids" were never really lost. Archaeologists knew about them. But when U.S. pilots in World War II (1939-45) spotted pyramid-shaped mounds near the city of Xian, the story sparked more interest.

Exploring the "pyramids" later led to the discovery of 38 burial mounds. The largest belonged to the first emperor of China, Qin Shi Huangdi. Ancient accounts said that the emperor's tomb was huge. It had taken more than 700,000 people to build it between 246 and 208 B.C. Inside, the chamber was modeled on the emperor's capital city, Xianyang.

The mounds may hold many archaeological treasures.

Imperial Tomb

The emperor was buried with many servants. They were sealed alive in the tomb, in order to serve their master in the **afterlife**.

In 1974, farmers dug up old remains near the emperor's tomb. In one of the mounds, **archaeologists** found an army of **terracotta** warriors standing guard over the tomb. There were more than 8,000 life-sized soldiers, together with chariots and horses.

Qin Shi Huangdi's tomb rises 250 feet (76 m) above the plain.

Mystery File: POISON PILLS

Qin Shi Huangdi's tomb has still not been opened. Experts want to wait until they have developed techniques to preserve its contents. Also, ancient accounts say that the tomb included rivers of mercury, which is highly poisonous.

Mystery words...

afterlife: in some religions, a place where people go after death

13

The Cave TEMPLES

In 1819, British army officers were hunting tigers in the jungles of central India, when they found a series of caves carved into a cliff. Inside the caves, they were amazed to find remarkable religious sculptures and paintings.

Statue of the Buddha in a carved cave

In all, the builders had carved 30 caves into a rock face hidden in a ravine near the village of Ajanta. From the statues and paintings, it was clear that the **monuments** had been dedicated to the Buddha, the founder of Buddhism. We now know that the caves had been built between 230 B.C. and 500 A.D. They were part of a Buddhist **monastery**. One of the caves featured a large hall for worship and a number of cells for the monks to sleep in.

Mystery words...

monuments: things built in remembrance of things from the past

14

Mysteriously Abandoned

After the monastery had been used for over 700 years, it was abandoned. New caves were left unfinished. The monks and the builders left, and the jungle grew back over the entrances. When it was found in the 19th century, everyone had forgotten it ever existed. Nobody knows why the caves were suddenly abandoned. It may be that Buddhism became less popular than India's other major religion, Hinduism.

Mystery File: ROCK BUILDING

Temples were carved into rock across India. It may have been easier than digging out rocks to make a stone building. The builders often carved the caves as if they were built of wood. For example, they carved roof beams that were not actually necessary in caves.

The caves are hidden deep in a jungle ravine.

Pools of MYSTERY

The Mayan civilization reached its height in Central America from about 250 to 900 A.D. On the Yucatán Peninsula of southern Mexico, the Maya worshiped mysterious caverns.

These flooded caverns are known as cenotes. The Maya believed they were gateways to the afterlife, the home of the dead. The **sinkholes** were created when limestone was eroded by the underground water that lies beneath much of the Yucatán Peninsula.

The cenotes were a key source of drinking water for the Maya

The Maya believed cenotes were gateways to the afterlife.

Some of the cenotes are like open pools. Others are dark wells that are lit only by a small opening overhead.

Sacred Sacrifice

To the ancient Maya, the cenotes were sacred. They threw valuable objects into the water. The Sacred Cenote is a pool outside the city of Chichen Itza. The Maya thought it was the home of the rain god. At the bottom of the pool, archaeologists have found weapons, tools, jewels, and carvings that were thrown in as **sacrifices** to the gods.

Mystery File: HUMAN SACRIFICE

Among other objects that have been found in the cenotes are human skeletons. It seems that the Maya sacrificed humans to their gods. They probably threw the victims in alive and left them to drown or starve in the caves.

Mystery words...

sacrifices: valuable things given as offerings to the gods

Homes in the CLIFFS

In the southwestern United States, ancient buildings perch beneath overhangs on tall cliffs. They were sheltered from the weather. Their location also protected them from enemies or wild animals.

The cliff-dwellers who built these hidden communities are known as the Anasazi or Pueblo. These Native peoples lived in the Southwest between about 1190 and 1260 A.D. At sites like Canyon de Chelly in Arizona and Mesa Verde in Colorado, they built homes from sandstone. The homes were joined to one another with doorways in the roofs. The only way in was by ladders, which could be pulled up as protection against an attack. The cities were built for defense.

Mystery words...
rituals: religious ceremonies that follow a fixed order of events

A Place for Rituals

The Pueblo monuments feature circular, half-buried pits. These are known as *kivas*. They were used for religious **rituals**, but no one is quite sure about their purpose. What little we know about the Pueblo peoples today comes from pottery they made or drawings they left on the walls. In the 13th century, the Pueblo peoples left their homes and migrated south and west, where their descendants still live.

Mystery File: CLIMATE CHANGE

Why were the cliff dwellings abandoned? Some experts believe that the climate changed in the 13th century. The Pueblo lands became drier, and their crops failed. No defenses could protect the people from that disaster.

Mesa Verde is home to dwellings and circular kivas.

Towns of GHOSTS

Hidden worlds are not always ancient. Around the world are more recent settlements that once flourished but which have since been abandoned. Today, the people who lived there are virtually forgotten.

A rusting car wreck in an old yard in Bodie, California

High in the hills east of the Sierra Nevada, in California, lie the ruins of Bodie. They stand alone along a dirt trail, miles from any highway. In 1876, gold was found nearby, and Bodie boomed. Up to 7,000 people arrived in a few years, and the town had 2,000 buildings. But the gold soon began to run out.

Mines were opened to dig for other **minerals**, but they closed one by one. By 1940, only 90 people still lived in Bodie. The buildings were rotting and abandoned. The streets that had once been full of miners and gunfighters were empty apart from tourists.

Abandoned buildings in the ghost town of Bodie, California

Mystery File: NEW GHOST TOWNS

Some ghost towns are abandoned before they are even occupied. Recently the Chinese built a number of cities they hoped would attract many people. But, due to the high costs to live in these cities, many have no residents.

Modern Ghost Towns

An even more recent ghost town is in Picher, Oklahoma. In 1996, scientists found that lead mines had contaminated the town's water supply. So the government bought the houses and moved everyone out.

Mystery words...

minerals: useful substances dug out of the ground by mining

Living UNDERGROUND

The mining town of Coober Pedy lies in one of the hottest parts of the Australian desert. To someone driving through, it looks like a small collection of huts. But below ground, nearly 2,000 residents live in special "**dugouts**."

Most of the people who live in Coober Pedy are miners. The town was founded early in the 20th century, when opal was discovered there. Opals are valuable gemstones that are often used in expensive jewelry. But conditions were hard for the miners who came to dig the opal.

At Coober Pedy, most of the town's life goes on underground.

Mystery words...

dugouts: shelters that are dug into the ground

Daytime temperatures in the summer often reach as high as 104°F (40°C). The miners dug homes into the hillsides around the town. They also built stores, bars, and churches underground. The earth keeps the rooms at a constant temperature, no matter how hot or cold it is outside. Today, Coober Pedy is known as one of the most unique places in Australia. It not only attracts opal miners, but tourists as well.

Building Underground

Underground buildings are used elsewhere, too. Beneath Toronto, Canada, the PATH network of tunnels forms the world's largest underground shopping mall. The tunnels protect residents from freezing winter temperatures and heavy snowfall.

Mystery File: SALT CARVING

Salt has been dug out of the Wieliczka mine in Poland since the 13th century. The miners began to carve religious statues deep in the mine. Eventually, they created dozens of statues, three chapels, and a whole cathedral underground.

Salt miners carved out chapels deep in the Wieliczka mine.

Life in the CAVES

Cappadocia is a hot, dry region of central Turkey. Its harsh, rocky environment does not have much wood to build with. Instead, the people who lived there carved homes into the remarkable rock formations.

The first underground buildings were made in the region in the eighth century B.C. Early Christians later built churches there; they used tunnels to avoid **persecution**. Their religion was illegal in the Roman Empire. The Romans often killed or arrested them.

The cave homes were important centers for early Christianity.

Mystery File:
CAVE DWELLERS

People who live in caves are known as troglodytes. Modern-day troglodytes live in caves in the West Bank, a Palestinian area of Israel. Near Granada in Spain, old cave dwellings have been renovated with electricity and running water.

The "fairy chimneys" are made of soft rock called tuff.

Cities Underground

The underground city of Kaymakli was linked by more than 100 tunnels. The town of Derinkuyu had enough tunnels to shelter 20,000 people and their animals. The best-known cave buildings are near Göreme. The soft rocks have been eroded into columns called "fairy chimneys." They were easy to hollow into homes and churches. Early Christians carved small cells for themselves where they could meditate without distraction.

Mystery words...

persecution: the ill-treatment of people based on race or religion

King Arthur's CAMELOT

In British legend, King Arthur ruled the kingdom from his castle at Camelot. Arthur gathered the Knights of the Round Table. They went on quests throughout the country, fighting for fairness and justice.

Many historians doubt that King Arthur existed, but other people think the stories were based on reality. They often try to find the location of Camelot. When Thomas Mallory wrote about King Arthur in the 15th century, he said Camelot was the castle at Winchester, in southern England. Winchester had a round table, like the one in

the story. But the Winchester table was made in the 14th century, 800 years after Arthur was supposed to have lived.

Cadbury Castle

Another suggested site of Camelot is Cadbury Castle. This hill fort stands near the Cam River in west England. Many nearby place names include the **syllable** "cam." Could this have been Camelot? Archaeologists dug at the site in the 1960s. They found a large fortification—but no evidence to link it to King Arthur and his famous knights.

The hill fort at Cadbury was dug into the top of the hill.

The ruins of Tintagel cling to a tiny island just off the coast.

Mystery File: TINTAGEL CASTLE

Arthur was said to have been born at Tintagel Castle. Today, the castle's ruins stand on rocks off the coast in Cornwall. In 1998, a stone was found there from the sixth century carved with the name "Artognou." Could it refer to the legendary king?

Mystery words...

syllable: a single unit of sounds that makes up a word

Monasteries of the MOUNTAINS

Buddhism began in India in the sixth century B.C. but by 1200 A.D. it was almost unknown in its homeland. Despite this, the faith was preserved in a few remote monasteries.

These monasteries were founded high in the Himalaya mountains. Few outsiders visited them. When the Islamic religion pushed Buddhism out of much of India, it did not reach mountain kingdoms such as Tibet.

Mystery words...

scriptures: the holy books on which a religion is based

The monasteries stood high on mountain ledges, or perched on the edges of ravines. The Tiger's Lair monastery in the Himalayan kingdom of Bhutan stands 2,300 feet (701 m) up a cliff face above the valley.

Saving the Faith

Safe in the monasteries, monks studied the teachings of the Buddha. They wrote down copies of Buddhists' holy **scriptures** and made sure that the faith survived. Eventually their efforts helped lead to a revival of Buddhism across the rest of India.

Mystery File: METÉORA MONKS

Monasteries have often been built in high places for defense. At Metéora, in Greece, six monasteries were built on top of natural pillars of rock. All building materials had to be lifted to the top. The monks were raised up in baskets.

The monasteries of the Himalayas were built to be easily defended.

Glossary

afterlife In some religions, the place where people go after death

ancestors The people from whom living people are descended

archaeologists People who investigate traces of the past

catacombs Underground cemeteries located in tunnels

dormitories Rooms where a number of people sleep

dugouts Shelters that are dug into the ground

gravity A force that attracts objects toward one another

minerals Useful substances dug out of the ground by mining

molten Melted, used to describe something that is usually solid

monastery A place for monks to live and worship in that is cut off from the everyday world

monuments Things made in remembrance of the past

outcrops Rock formations that stick out of the ground

persecution The ill-treatment of people based on race or religion

rituals Religious ceremonies that follow a fixed order of events

sacrifices Valuable things given as offerings to the gods

scriptures The holy books on which a religion is based

sinkholes Holes worn in the ground that let water flow into underground passages

syllable A single unit of sounds that makes up a word

terracotta A type of pottery made from hardened clay

Find Out More

BOOKS

Capek, Michael. *Easter Island* (Unearthing Ancient Worlds). Twenty-First Century Books, 2008.

Capek, Michael. *Emperor Qin's Terra Cotta Army* (Unearthing Ancient Worlds). Twenty-First Century Books, 2007.

Croy, Anita. *Ancient Pueblo* (National Geographic Investigates). National Geographic Children's Books, 2009.

Harris, Nathaniel. *Ancient Maya* (National Geographic Investigates). National Geographic Children's Books, 2009.

Parvis, Sarah E. *Ghost Towns* (Scary Places). Bearport Publishing, 2008.

WEBSITES

Remote mountain monasteries
Environmental Graffiti list of the world's cliff-top monasteries
www.environmentalgraffiti.com/featured/most-beautiful-precariously-placed-monasteries/17786

Cappadocia
New York Times slideshow of the home of Turkey's cave dwellers
www.nytimes.com/slideshow/2007/09/05/travel/20070909_NEXT_SLIDESHOW_index.html

Ghost towns
Weburbanist directory of ancient and modern ghost towns
http://weburbanist.com/2008/10/19/ghost-town-abandoned-city-examples-images/

Index

A Journey to the Centre of the Earth 9
afterlife 13, 16
Ajanta Caves 14–15
Anasazi 18–19
Arthur, King 26–27
Australia 22–23

Bhutan 29
Bodie 20, 21
Britain 26–27
Buddhism 14–15, 28–29

Cadbury Castle 27
California 20–21
Camelot 26–27
Canyon de Chelly 18
Cappadocia 24–25
catacombs 11
caves 14–15, 16–17, 24–25
cenotes 16–17
Central America 16–17
China 12–13, 21
Christians 24, 25
Coober Pedy 22–23

Earth, hollow 8–9
Easter Island 6–7

"fairy chimneys" 24, 25
First Emperor 12–13
France 4–5, 11

ghost towns 20–21
Göreme 25
Granada 25
Greeks, ancient 8

Himalaya 28, 29
hollow Earth theory 8–9
human sacrifice 17

India 14–15, 28

King Arthur 26–27
kivas 19

Lascaux caves 4–5

Mallory, Thomas 26
Maya 16–17
Mesa Verde 18, 19
Metéora 29
Mexico 16–17
mining 21, 22–23
moai 6, 7
monasteries 14, 15, 28–29

Navajo 8
North Pole 9

opal 22

Paris 11
Picher, Oklahoma 21

Poland 22, 23
Pueblo 18–19
pyramids 12, 13

Qin Shi Huangdi 12–13

rock-cut temples 15
Roggeveen, Jacob 6–7

sacrifice 17
Saigon 10
Symmes, John Cleves 9

terracotta warriors 13
Tiger's Lair 28, 29
Tintagel Castle 26–27
tombs 12, 13
Toronto 23
troglodytes 25
tunnels 10–11
Turkey 24, 25

United States 18–19, 20–21

Verne, Jules 9
Viet Cong 10, 11
Vietnam War 10–11
Wieliczka mine 22, 23
Winchester 26–27

Yucatán Peninsula 16–17